Dear Parent:
Your child's love of reading starts here!

Every child learns to read in a different way and at his or her own speed. Some go back and forth between reading levels and read favorite books again and again. Others read through each level in order. You can help your young reader improve and become more confident by encouraging his or her own interests and abilities. From books your child reads with you to the first books he or she reads alone, there are I Can Read Books for every stage of reading:

SHARED READING
Basic language, word repetition, and whimsical illustrations, ideal for sharing with your emergent reader

BEGINNING READING
Short sentences, familiar words, and simple concepts for children eager to read on their own

READING WITH HELP
Engaging stories, longer sentences, and language play for developing readers

READING ALONE
Complex plots, challenging vocabulary, and high-interest topics for the independent reader

I Can Read Books have introduced children to the joy of reading since 1957. Featuring award-winning authors and illustrators and a fabulous cast of beloved characters, I Can Read Books set the standard for beginning readers.

A lifetime of discovery begins with the   d!"

Visit www.icanread.com
on enriching your child's rea   ⸺⸺ience.

ISBN 978-0-06-290742-4

20 21 22 23 24 SCP 10 9 8 7 6 5 4 3 2 1 ❖ First Edition

SHARK SURF SURPRISE

Adapted by Steve Foxe
Based on the episode "Shark Surf Surprise"
by Louise Moon

HARPER
An Imprint of HarperCollinsPublishers

I am Jett.

Sometimes I'm a plane.

Sometimes I'm a robot.

I take boxes across the world.
This box is going to Australia.

"I'm Jett!" I say.

"I'm on time, every time.
This box is for you."

"Thanks, Jett!" the girl says.
"It's my first surfboard!"

"Can you show me
how to surf?"
the girl asks.

"I can't," I say.

"But I know who can!"

I call Mira and Swampy.

They know how to surf!

We paddle out into the water.

Mira hops up onto
the board.

She shows the girl
how to ride the wave!
"I'm doing it!" the girl says.

"I'm ready to give it a try,"
I say.

Oh no!

What's that behind us?

It's a shark!
Swim faster!

"Did the shark swim away?"
Mira asks.
"I don't see it underwater."

"The shark swam past us!"
I say.
"Time to go turbo!"

Whoa!

There is something

under the water.

It's Willy!

"Need some help?"

he asks.

"Just in time!" I say.
Willy gives everyone a ride
on his back.

Oh no!
Willy gives the shark
a ride too!

"Hold on," the girl says.
"The shark isn't hungry.
He's hurt!"

"You're right," I say.
"He's got something
stuck in his teeth!"

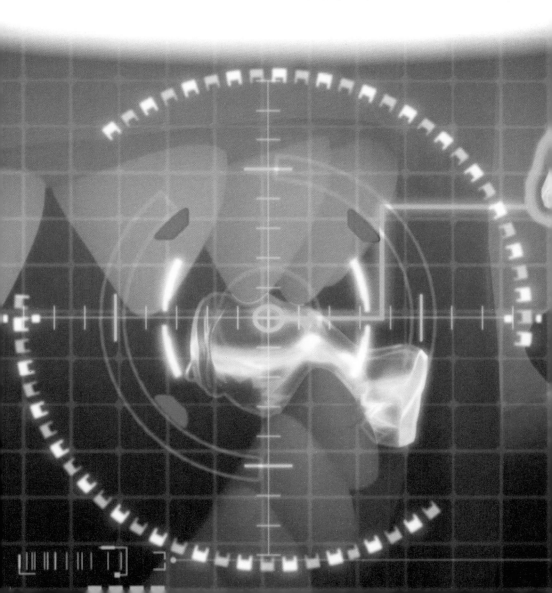

I use my claw tool
to help the shark.

"Now everyone can surf!"
the girl says.

The Super Wings

save the day again!

"All better!" I say.

The shark looks
much happier!